Jamie O'Rourke
and the
POOKA

by

TOMIE dePAOLA

SCHOLASTIC INC.
New York Toronto London Auckland Sydney
Mexico City New Delhi Hong Kong

For my two Irish buddies,
John Sullivan and Kim "O'Sutherland"

ISBN 0-439-27614-4

Copyright © 2000 by Tomie dePaola. All rights reserved.
Published by Scholastic Inc., 555 Broadway, New York, NY 10012,
by arrangement with Penguin Putnam Inc. SCHOLASTIC and associated
logos are trademarks and/or registered trademarks of Scholastic Inc.

12 11 10 9 8 7 6   2 3 4 5 6/0

Printed in the U.S.A.   08

First Scholastic printing, January 2001

Designed by Marikka Tamura. Text set in Aurelia Book.
The paintings for this book were done with liquid acrylic on handmade Fabriano paper.

Jamie O'Rourke," Eileen said. "Wake up. I've something to tell you."

Jamie, who was the laziest man in all of Ireland, was sleeping in the warm sun outside their cottage. His wife gave him a shake.

"Wake up, wake up, for heaven's sake," Eileen said again.

"I'm not sleeping," Jamie answered with a yawn. "Sure, I was sittin' here thinkin'."

"Now, Jamie, please listen," Eileen replied. "Do you remember that I'm going up to visit my sister Kathleen and her family to help with the new baby?"

Jamie let out a snore.

Eileen poked him.

"What are ye doing, woman? Can't you see I'm right in the middle of solvin' a great problem?" Jamie answered. "Well, now that all the fine thoughts I was havin' have clear flown out of me head, you might as well tell me what's goin' on."

Eileen explained to Jamie (for the fortieth time, most likely) that she was off to Kathleen's and would be there for the better part of a week.

"Now," Eileen went on, "I've cleaned the cottage from top to bottom. I've cooked all kinds of good things and put them in the larder. All you'll have to do is the washin' up each night and give a quick swipe of the broom every now and then."

"Well, well, me darlin', you're too good for the likes of me,"
Jamie said. "But don't you be worryin'. I'll take good care of
everything so's you won't even know you've been away. Now,
give us a kiss and be off with you."

Down the road went Eileen O'Rourke.

"All of this commotion has made me as tired as a farmer plowin' five fields," Jamie said to himself. "I think I'll just have me a lie-down. And sure, isn't that a sweet idea? If I stay in bed and only get up for a bite, I'll not be dirtyin' a thing." So Jamie O'Rourke climbed into bed, even though the sun was high in the sky, and fell fast asleep.

"Jamie, Jamie O'Rourke," three voices called outside the door. "Where are ye, man? We heard Eileen's off to her sister's, so's we have come to keep ye company."

Jamie woke up and recognized the voices of his cronies, Patrick, Michael, and Seamus. Jamie got out of bed (and since he hadn't taken off his clothes, he didn't have to be putting them on again).

"Come in, come in, lads," Jamie said, opening the door. The sun was sinking behind the hills.

"Well, what do we have here?" Jamie asked, pointing at a crockery jug.

"This is the finest cider you'll taste this side of the county," Patrick said.

"Get some mugs," Michael said.

"And some grub," Seamus said. He knew that Eileen wouldn't leave Jamie without plenty of good things to eat.

When the food was on the table, and mugs, plates, and knives and forks too, they all sat down.

They had themselves a fine old time, laughing and eating until it was time to go home.

"Well," the three friends told Jamie, "we'll be headin' down the hill, and you'll be wantin' to get your rest, Jamie. Tomorrow you'll be havin' a busy mornin' cleanin' up all this mess."

"Aye, that's the truth, lads," Jamie said, looking around. But the mere sight of the messy cottage made him the most tired man in all of Ireland, as well as the laziest. So he went to bed.

Jamie was fast asleep when a noise woke him. It was the sound of the cottage door and the clatter of hooves on the stone floor. Jamie opened one eye and took a peek.

And what a sight he saw! He couldn't tell if it was a man or a donkey standing there. Whatever it was, it had long ears and a tail.

"Saints preserve us," Jamie whispered.

"I may as well begin first as last," the creature, who was a pooka, said out loud to himself.

He stirred the fire, poured some water into a big pot, and put it on the fire. As soon as the water was hot, the pooka washed the dishes, the mugs, and the cutlery. He put the leftovers in proper dishes and back into the larder. He swept the floor and gave the fire a good raking.

Then the pooka left the house with such a slam of the door, Jamie nearly fell out of bed.

The next evening when Patrick, Michael, and Seamus
came by with a fresh jug of cider, they were amazed to see
the cottage as if Eileen had been there.

"How did this all happen?" they asked.

"Well, me lads," Jamie replied, "I got up with the birds and
cleaned it all up just like any good husband would do when
his darlin' wife is away."

Patrick, Michael, and Seamus looked at each other. They didn't really believe Jamie, but there it was. So the four friends had another grand time just like the night before.

When his friends had gone, leaving even more of a mess, Jamie climbed into bed. But instead of falling asleep, he waited under the covers. Sure enough, the door opened and the pooka was back, cleaning up everything fast and furiously.

"This is luck indeed," Jamie said to himself. "Why, with this creature comin' and cleanin' up, I can have me cronies here every night—every night, that is, until Eileen comes home."

And that is what he did. Night after night, Jamie, Patrick, Michael, and Seamus had a grand old time, making a grand old mess. And every night, the pooka came in and set things to right.

By the end of the week, Jamie was curious about this accommodating creature. So he decided to stay up and have a chat with him. He was a little scared when the pooka came in and went right to the fire. But he took a deep breath, swallowed a mouthful of cider for courage, and spoke up.

"Now then, sir, if I'm not takin' a liberty, might I be knowin' who you are and why you are so kind as to do the cleanin' up each night after me friends and meself?"

The pooka turned and looked at Jamie. "I'll tell you, and you're welcome to it. A long time back, I was the laziest servant that ever was clothed and fed, and did no work for it. When my time came for the other world, this is the punishment I was given for my lazy ways—to find a place each night to labor in.

"As I was wanderin' by the other night, I looked in the window of your cottage. As sure as can be, you needed my help. It's not so bad, for at least I'm out of the cold, but when I finish my work, the saints preserve us, that cold wind goes right through me bones. It wouldn't be so hard if I had me a nice warm coat."

Well, well, Jamie thought. *I can probably help the poor creature out.*
The next night, after his friends left, Jamie sat and waited for the pooka. Eileen would be home tomorrow, but Jamie wasn't worried. He knew the pooka would do an excellent job of cleaning up, especially when Jamie gave him the old coat he had pulled from the trunk.

As soon as the pooka came in, Jamie showed him the coat. He helped him into it and buttoned it up. The pooka went to the mirror. He was most pleased with what he saw.

"I am much obliged to you, Jamie O'Rourke. You have made me happy at last. Now, I'll be sayin' good night to you." The pooka turned to go.

"Wait, wait," Jamie cried out. "You're leavin' too soon. What about the washin' up and the sweepin'?"

"Ah," the pooka said, "now it's your turn. My punishment was only to last until some kind creature like yourself liked the way I'd done my duty and rewarded me for it. Good-bye, and you'll see no more of me."

The pooka left, and there was Jamie with the mess. Or should we say Eileen? For when she arrived the next morning and looked around the cottage, she said, "Oh, Jamie O'Rourke. What do you have to say for yourself?"

But Jamie said nothing. He was too busy thinking he shouldn't have been in such a hurry to reward that ungrateful pooka!

AUTHOR'S NOTE

Jamie O'Rourke is back! This time he's joined not only by his wife Eileen and his cronies, Patrick, Michael, and Seamus, but by a pooka.

Now, according to William Butler Yeats, who collected, edited, and published many Irish folktales, a pooka (also spelled *puca*) is an animal spirit who lives a solitary life. Some people think that the word *pooka* comes from the Gallic word *poc*—a he-goat. Others also think that a pooka is the forefather of Shakespeare's Puck.

Pookas come in many forms—a horse, a he-goat, an ass, a bull, even an eagle. (One of the most famous pookas is Harvey, the ubiquitous friend of Jimmy Stewart in the play and the movie of the same name.)

Our pooka was once a very lazy man who, when his time came for the other world, was given a punishment for his lazy ways. He had to come back to earth as a pooka and make up all the work he failed to do when he was alive.

So, watch out, Jamie O'Rourke!

—TdeP N. H.